D1315447

Sun Jack &
Rain Jack

For a free color catalog describing Gareth Stevens' list of high-quality books, call 1-800-341-3569 (USA) or 1-800-461-9120 (Canada).

ISBN 0-8368-1089-9

This edition first published in 1994 by
Gareth Stevens Publishing
1555 North RiverCenter Drive, Suite 201
Milwaukee, Wisconsin 53212, USA

This edition first published in 1994 by Gareth Stevens, Inc. Original edition first published in Germany under the title S*ONNEN-JAN/REGEN-JAN,* © 1993 Verlag Heinrich Ellerman München.

Ursel Scheffler has a Master of Arts degree and has been writing for children since her first published children's book in 1975. In addition to writing picture books and fairy tales, Ms. Scheffler also writes fiction for older children. Her 100th original title is to be released this year.

Jutta Timm was a graphic designer in advertising before working with children's books. Since 1983, she has been illustrating children's books for various publishing houses in Germany.

Dave Morice is a writer, poet, and illustrator, and is currently Guest Lecturer in Children's Literature at the University of Iowa—Iowa City. Among his publications are three children's books: *Dot Town, The Happy Birthday Handbook,* and *A Visit from St. Alphabet.*

Printed in the United States of America
1 2 3 4 5 6 7 8 9 99 98 97 96 95 94

At this time, Gareth Stevens, Inc., does not use 100 percent recycled paper, although the paper used in our books does contain about 30 percent recycled fiber. This decision was made after a careful study of current recycling procedures revealed their dubious environmental benefits. We will continue to explore recycling options.

Sun Jack &
Rain Jack

Written by Ursel Scheffler
Illustrations by Jutta Timm
English text by Dave Morice

· · · · · · · · · · · ·

Gareth Stevens Publishing
MILWAUKEE

A rainy day, and Jack is happy.
He loves to play in the rain.
He builds a dam, he launches ships,
Upon the bounding main.

A rainy day, and Jack is happy.
He loves to walk in the rain.
He sloshes through the soggy streets
And down the slippery lane.

9

A rainy day, and Jack is happy.
He loves to jump in the rain
And hop through sidewalk puddles
To splash his best friend, Jane.

A rainy day, and Jack is happy.
He loves to look at the rain,
To watch it fall and soak the world
Beyond the window pane.

A rainy day, and Jack is happy,
'Cause when he stays inside,
His grandad tells him wondrous tales
Till dreams become his guide.

A rainy day, and Jack is happy; but when it's sunny, he still feels snappy!

A sunny day, and Jack is happy; but when it rains, he still feels snappy

A sunny day, and Jack is happy.
His dad gives him a ride.
His puppy frolics in the grass,
And Kitty tries to hide.

14

A sunny day, and Jack is happy.
He rows his little boat
Past sister Kitty and their dad,
Who work to keep afloat!

11

A sunny day, and Jack is happy.
He takes a long, long walk.
He swings and plays with all his friends
And joins in sandbox talk.

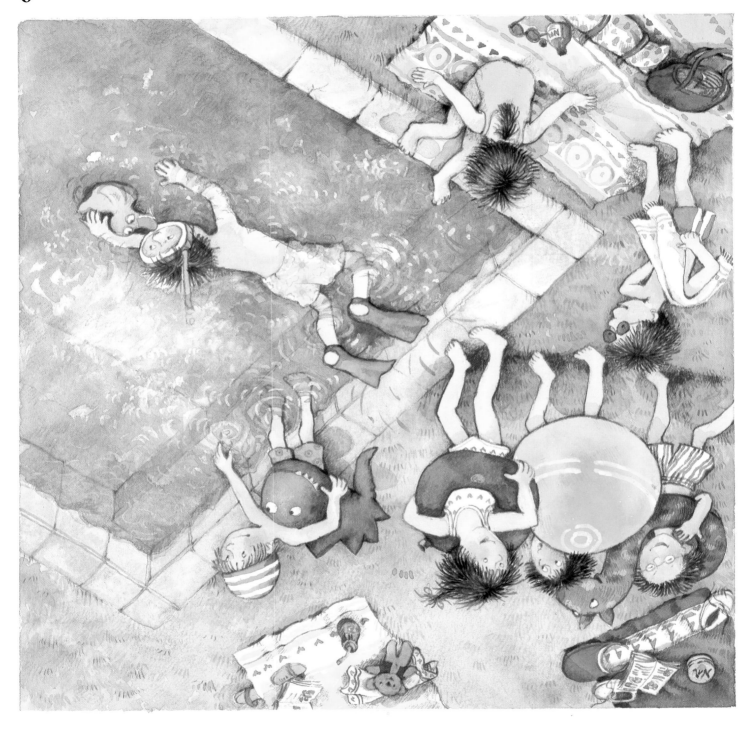

A sunny day, and Jack is happy.
He snorkels in the pool.
It's hot outside, but not too hot.
The water feels so cool!

A sunny day, and Jack is happy.

He loves to go outside

And race his shiny tricycle

On a wild, adventurous ride.

Sun Jack

& Rain Jack

Written by Ursel Scheffler
Illustrations by Jutta Timm
English text by Dave Morice

· · · · · · · · · · · ·

Gareth Stevens Publishing
MILWAUKEE

For a free color catalog describing Gareth Stevens' list of high-quality books, call 1-800-341-3569 (USA) or 1-800-461-9120 (Canada).

ISBN 0-8368-1089-9

This edition first published in 1994 by
Gareth Stevens Publishing
1555 North RiverCenter Drive, Suite 201
Milwaukee, Wisconsin 53212, USA

This edition first published in 1994 by Gareth Stevens, Inc. Original edition first published in Germany under the title S*ONNEN-JAN/REGEN-JAN,* © 1993 Verlag Heinrich Ellerman München.

Ursel Scheffler has a Master of Arts degree and has been writing for children since her first published children's book in 1975. In addition to writing picture books and fairy tales, Ms. Scheffler also writes fiction for older children. Her 100th original title is to be released this year.

Jutta Timm was a graphic designer in advertising before working with children's books. Since 1983, she has been illustrating children's books for various publishing houses in Germany.

Dave Morice is a writer, poet, and illustrator, and is currently Guest Lecturer in Children's Literature at the University of Iowa—Iowa City. Among his publications are three children's books: *Dot Town, The Happy Birthday Handbook,* and *A Visit from St. Alphabet.*

Printed in the United States of America
1 2 3 4 5 6 7 8 9 99 98 97 96 95 94

Sun Jack

& Rain Jack